Going to HELL

5 Horror Stories

Rebecca M. Senese

Other Books by Rebecca M. Senese

The Night Killers

The Colour of Blood: The Chronicles of Richard Damon

Wreck the Halls: 5 Christmas Horror Stories

Oh the Horror! 5 Horror Stories

By Howl & Claw: 5 Werewolf Stories

With a Bite: 5 Vampire Tales

In Dwarf Land and Cannibal Country

A Very Zombie Christmas

The Beginners Guide to the Recently Deceased

Daily Bread

The In-Between Series
Book 1: A Reluctance of Blood
Book 2: A Remembrance of Flesh
*Book 3: A Retribution of Soul

*Forthcoming

Going to HELL

5 Horror Stories

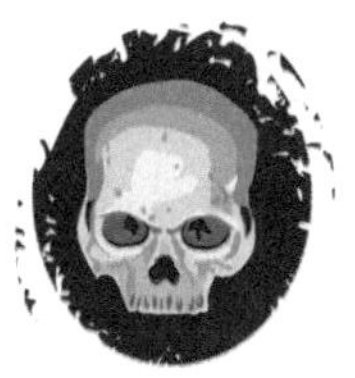

Rebecca M. Senese

RFAR PUBLISHING
TORONTO, CANADA

Published 2014 by RFAR Publishing
Toronto, Canada
http://www.RFARPublishing.com

This is a work of fiction. All characters appearing in this work are fictitious. Any resemblance to real persons, living or dear is purely coincidental.

Trade paper edition designed by Rebecca M. Senese
in InDesign CS5.5

Electronic editions designed by Rebecca M. Senese

Cover design: Rebecca M. Senese
Cover Image © DanFLCreativo / CanStockPhoto.com
Interior Images © pashtet8286 / DepositPhotos.com
angelp / CanStockPhoto.com

ISBN: 978-1-927603-23-9

Publications Acknowledgement

"Old MacDonald Had a Farm." First published in *Deadbolt Magazine*, 1999.

"Wild Call." First published in the *World Fantasy Convention CD-ROM*, 2001.

"Writing Critique." First published in *Just Write*, 1994, and reprinted in *Calliope*, 1999.

Going to HELL

5 Horror Stories

Table of Contents

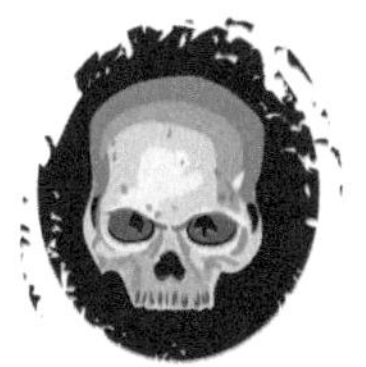

INTRODUCTION

Welcome to my *Going to Hell* compilation! I've named this compilation after a comment I received from a critique of one of these stories. The reader found my story offensive and horrible. To her, I was going to hell for what I'd written and she was happy to tell me. Talk about a reaction! For a horror writer, such a strident objection is like music. The worst thing for a horror writer, or any writer for that matter, is apathy.

So I welcome you to visit a few tales that might be a trifle disturbing. Just remember to keep the lights on bright. Watch out for little chickies or gargoyles. Wait, was that a wolf howl? Be careful of that filing cabinet. Don't get a paper cut. Look out for the shadows. They move...

Rebecca M. Senese
December 2013

Old MacDonald Had A Farm

"Them little chickies, them little chickies," the farmer murmured as he walked away from the pen. Behind him the animals rattled against the fence, as if to draw him back, but he wearily shook his head.

"Them little chickies," he murmured again, stepping into the barn. Placing the feed bag on the ground, he pulled out a handkerchief and mopped his brow. The weather had been damned hot all day, that was for sure. They were in for a storm, yes sir, and a hell of a one at that. Just looking at the clouds, he could tell. Despite the last meager rays of the setting sun, the clouds were the colour of grey mud, hanging in the sky like fists ready to pound the ground. Then the storm would come ripping down, bringing torrents of rain and wind.

He'd have to take the chickies into the barn before then but there would be time. Storm wouldn't hit until ten or so. He hoped Kogan, the company man, would arrive before then. The chickies looked their best outside.

Behind him he heard the chickies scrabbling over the food, squawking at each other. Lordy, they made a hell of a racket. A good thing his farm was well away from the road. Wouldn't want to be having that racket out where folks could hear it. Might bother their dinners or something.

He stood listening to the sound of them a moment longer. They sounded healthy and strong. Best batch yet. His old chest inflated with pride. He'd been breeding them little chickies for a long time now, longer than anybody. Won first prize at the fair only a month before. Everybody commented on how sweet and juicy his little chickie nuggets tasted. Mouth watering. He'd hung that blue ribbon up in the living room over the mantle. A place of honour.

And he remembered Kogan, the company man, wearing a steel gray suit looking like he was some kind of alien creature come down to earth like the ones in the newspapers in the grocery store. Came up to the farmer after he won first prize, surrounded by all the other farmers, came just to shake his hand. Said he was from Down-Home Families and could they have a word.

Down-Home Families. His head'd been spinning. They was famous. He'd seen their restaurants in town when he visited, although he'd never been inside one himself. Never went in for that fancy stuff, but Mr. Kogan didn't seem to mind that. He was more interested in the chickies.

The farmer picked up the feed bag and trudged back into the house. He stowed the bag in the pantry under the stairs and stepped over to the sink. Turning on the tap, he let the water run over his hands, sighing at the feel of it. Nice and cool today, yep it was going to rain. His hands seemed to hurt more these days. Just getting old, he thought. He picked up the soap and started scrubbing.

When he entered the living room he saw the fan was still on, pointed at his favourite chair. He smiled a little and settled down into the cushions. The chair was old and faded, much like himself, he thought. But they were both comfortable.

The cool air felt good against his skin. It was so humid and hot. It made his old bones ache, to be so humid. Maybe it was time to pick up roots and move down south like old Jed Winslow. If this Kogan fellow liked his chickies enough he could afford to move. Leave the farm behind, not that he wouldn't miss it, oh of course he would. But he'd been working hard all his life. He deserved a rest.

"What do you think of the south, Muriel?" he asked his wife. She sat on the couch, knitting. She didn't answer. She never answered, never looked up. She didn't seem to notice him after her accident. Falling head first down the cellar stairs had given her a nasty lump on the head. The doctors said she would have to go to some clinic but he refused to send her. She did just fine here. She knitted and cooked and cleaned like always, even if she did do it at weird times. So what if she vacuumed at three in the morning, or made dinner at eleven in the morning and breakfast at eight in the evening? No one had to live with it but him.

So he didn't expect her to answer, he just liked to hear his own voice once in a while. Their boy had moved to the city, hadn't wanted to be a farmer, didn't like his father's techniques. There was no one else to talk to except the chickies and talking to them was a little like going mad. He wasn't mad, no sir.

In fact, he rather liked it this way. He got his meals, all mixed up and strange, but he didn't have to put up with her yammering. The house stayed mostly clean, although she seemed to consistently miss parts of it, like the hallway. The dust in there was like a desert.

He glanced at his watch. Mr. Kogan was due to arrive soon. The farmer hefted himself out of the chair with a grunt.

"Got to clean up a bit here, Muriel," he told his wife. As if it was a cue, she set down her knitting and stood up, turning toward the stairs. The farmer watched without curiosity. She probably thought it was bed time or something. That was just as well, couldn't do to have Mr. Kogan see her. He probably wouldn't understand.

He tidied up around the living room, straightening the magazines and fluffing the pillows. The hallway could not stay as it was so he took out a broom and set about taming the desert. Yep, there was still hard wood underneath it all when he was done.

Next he tidied the kitchen, setting the breakfast dishes into the sink to soak. Really they were lunch dishes; Muriel had made roast beef at eleven in the morning. Mighty tasty it was. He'd had a couple good sized helpings and put the rest in the fridge for future lunches.

But Mr. Kogan was coming to take a look at the chickies. Excitement grew in his belly. He finished up in the kitchen, wiping his hands on the front of his overalls. Surveying his work, he nodded in satisfaction. Everything looked fine. Now he would have one last look at the chickies.

The rain hadn't started yet when he stepped outside, but the clouds looked even lower in the sky and more ominous. The sun had all but disappeared, the last dying rays still fighting against the advancing black clouds. The farmer ignored them and strolled towards the chicken coop. It was still oppressively hot but hopefully the rain would drain some of the heat away.

The chickies started rustling about on his approach, kicking up dust with their feet. Probably think it's feeding time, he thought and chuckled. Hell, they only got fed a little while ago. Damn things would eat 'til they exploded if he let them.

"Hush, little chickies, hush, hush," he said soothingly. They rustled about behind the wire, pressing their faces forward. A few of them squawked, clawing at the wire, and that started them all squawking. He watched them with an amused grin. Yep, they were lusty and strong, just perfect for Down-Home Families.

"You gonna make me rich," the farmer said. "Gonna sell you to the Down-Home Families folks. Nice plump little chickies going to be leaving soon."

The chickies squawked even louder and began banging against the fence. The farmer shook his finger at them in a warning gesture.

"Now you be good chickies when Mr. Kogan gets here. Show your best behaviours." Best get changed, he thought, that company man'll be here soon. He turned away and started back towards the house. Behind him the chickies were making all kinds of racket. He chuckled himself; sometimes he could swear the things understood him.

Once back inside, he headed for the stairs. He stripped off his old worn overalls and picked out a new pair. They were clean and crisp, hardly ever worn these overalls. Yep, they looked mighty spiffy. In the bathroom, he washed his face and hands. A quick look at his chin told him he didn't need to shave again. He polished up his glasses and was ready.

Behind him on the bed, Muriel stirred, murmuring incoherently. The farmer walked over to stand beside her and patted her arm.

"You sleep well, Muriel," he whispered. "I'll tell you all about it when Mr. Kogan buys the chickies."

She didn't stir again so he left the bedroom, closing and locking the door behind him. It was the only way he could be sure Muriel would stay put. He pocketed the key and headed downstairs.

The fan was still going so he sat down to wait. He wanted to keep cool, no use changing if he sweated like a pig and looked terrible by the time that company man showed up. That wouldn't do to meet Mr. Kogan.

He imagined that Kogan probably lived in the city and wore expensive clothes, like the suit he'd worn to the fair. Probably drove one of those souped up cars and had lots of ladies hanging on his arm. Can't be more than thirty, I'll bet, the farmer thought, recalling the smooth face behind the steel rimmed sunglasses, and never did an honest day's work with his hands in his life. But that didn't matter. Kogan was coming to look at the chickies and make a deal.

Suddenly there was a loud thunderclap overhead, surprising the farmer. A few seconds later a flash of lightning burst out across the sky. The farmer got up from his chair and crossed to the window. The clouds were much darker. Even as he watched a few drops were starting to fall. Too late to take in the chickies without making himself a mess. Just have to leave them in the rain and show them to Kogan that way.

He sighed, hoped the rain would hold off a little longer.

A car appeared in the distance, drawing closer with each second. It was large and white, and seemed to shine even in the dullness of the approaching storm. The farmer caught his breath, feeling his heart pound with excitement. It was the Down-Home Families fella!

He stepped away from the window and quickly checked himself over. He seemed fine and the place looked respectable. Nervously he brushed at his overalls and walked over to the front door, flicking on the porch light.

Don't be opening the door right away, he told himself, don't wanta appear too anxious, don't want him to know how nervous I am.

He could hear the car now over the occasional thunderclap. The murmur of its engine was a constant buzz against the fury of the rising storm. As it drew into the driveway, the farmer opened the door and stepped out to meet it.

The car rolled to a smooth stop and one of the back doors opened. Kogan stepped out, looking as immaculately dressed as he had at the fair.

He wore a steel gray suit that seemed to ripple in the rising wind. The colour of it was oddly out of place here, better suited to board rooms and conference tables than an old farm like this. Kogan carried a silver briefcase in one hand and held out the other to the farmer.

"It's good to see you again, Mr. Jenkins," he said smoothly.

"Come in out of the rain, Mr. Kogan," the farmer said. He held the door open for the company man to step inside.

"Please have a seat, Mr. Kogan." The farmer gestured to the couch. As Kogan crossed to the couch and sat down the farmer felt a rush of embarrassment. Beside the company man's polished suit, his house seemed dull and tacky. He hunched his shoulders in despair as he retreated to his favourite armchair. How could he ever hope to impress this shining company man? His chickies probably would be one of hundreds that he saw every day. Nothing special.

But Kogan was nodding. "You have a very comfortable home," he said smoothly. The farmer looked up quickly to see if the man was making fun of him but there was no humour on the company fella's face.

"Shall we get down to business, Mr. Jenkins?" Kogan said. He placed his briefcase squarely on the coffee table and flipped it open.

"Oh, yes, sir," the farmer said. He relaxed a little. Maybe things would work out just fine, he was just nervous was all.

Kogan pulled out some papers and set them on the coffee table in front of the farmer. "These are standard inspection clauses that you must sign. It allows us access to your chickies and let's us run some quality control tests, just to make sure your breeding is true and that the fine quality I tasted at the fair wasn't just a fluke." He smiled reassuringly, his cheeks shining. The farmer nodded eagerly.

"Now if we agree to buy your chickies, Mr. Jenkins, we will attain all rights to them. That means that you can't raise any chickies with these characteristics. In fact, it is a Down-Home Families policy to ask that you not engage in any direct competition, which means we would prefer you to get out of breeding chickies entirely." He paused and smiled his plastic smile again. "Of course, with the money you'll be receiving I imagine you could find plenty of things to fill your time."

"Oh, I'm sure I could, Mr. Kogan," the farmer said eagerly. "I wouldn't miss it all that much. Been lots of things I've been wanting doing."

"And now you'll have the time and resources to do them, Mr. Jenkins," Kogan said, enthusiastically. He tapped the papers. "Please have a read through these and sign at the bottom. Then we can take a peak at your chickies and I can arrange to have one of our teams pick some up for testing. And we can get this show on the road."

The farmer beamed and picked up the papers. They were long, filled with densely packed words like "therein" and "herefore" and "nevertheless." He read as much as he could, gleaning the gist of the agreement out of it. There was a lot of insistence that the chickies be his to sell along with the breeding of them. It took a lot of words for them to say that simple thing, but who was he to judge? As long as they bought his little chickies for the Down-Home Families restaurants they could use up as many fancy words as they liked.

He signed where Kogan showed him and passed the papers back. They disappeared into the briefcase which closed with a sharp click. Kogan smiled. "Let's go see those chickies, shall we?"

"Right this way, Mr. Kogan." The farmer stood up and led him through the kitchen to the back door. He was happy to see that the rain had held off. Thunder and lightning still chased each other across the sky, with the occasional raindrop as accompaniment, but the storm hadn't started. Should hold off until they were finished looking at the chickies.

The farmer held the door open for Kogan and then led him past the barn towards the coop. During the quiet moments between thunder claps, the farmer could hear the chickies squawking their protests. The sound of their voices made him stand a little straighter. Even if by some fluke this company man didn't like his chickies, he knew they were the best in the county. And there were no one who could tell him different.

They rounded the corner of the barn and the coop came into view. The chickies reacted as they saw him, clambering for attention as always. The farmer chuckled aloud. He turned to comment to Kogan.

Kogan had turned the corner of the barn and stopped. His mouth hung open, his suit looked wrinkled and dull. His face was the colour of blanched milk. He blinked as if to stop his eyes from watering.

The farmer stepped toward him, concerned. "Mr. Kogan, are you alright?"

Kogan took a step and pointed past the farmer, toward the coop. "Those... those are your little chickies?" he whispered.

The farmer swelled with pride. "Oh yes, sir," he said loudly. "These are the best little chickies in the county." The chickies squawked in acknowledgement.

Kogan's face turned even whiter and he bolted for the back of the barn. The farmer ran after him, alarmed. Goodness, what could be the matter? Hadn't the man ever seen chickies in a coop before?

He came across Kogan kneeling on the ground, his suit streaked with dirt. The farmer touched his shoulder and Kogan started, looking up with wild eyes.

"Mr. Kogan, are you alright?" the farmer repeated.

Kogan struggled to his feet, wiping his mouth. The farmer suddenly saw that the man had thrown up. Good heavens, he thought, the poor man is sick. He took Kogan's arm to steer him toward the house.

"Those are your chickies?" Kogan said. His voice came close to a shriek. "Those are what you won first prize for at the fair?"

"Yes sir, they are. I won't be lying to you."

Kogan swallowed. "I ate some of your little chickies," he said. His face grew pale again.

"Mighty tasty, weren't they?" the farmer said. "Folks can't get enough. My chickie burgers have been popular around these parts for years. Everyone wants some of my little chickies. A sweeter, more tender meat you'll never find, I reckon."

Kogan stared at him for a moment, speechless. He wiped his mouth again. "You say people have been tasting your chickies for years?"

"Yep, best in the county. Even made the governor a burger out of my chickie meat once.

He said it was delicious and asked me if he could buy some to take home. I only had a little of it with me, but he made me a fine offer. Said he would be happy for more whenever I could oblige him. Now once a year I send him a batch of my special chickie burgers. He tries to pay but I'm proud to have them served up for the governor."

"The governor," Kogan whispered.

"Oh yes." The farmer was warming up to the subject. He loved to talk about his little chickies. "Peoples are always asking me my secret and trying to buy them. Fact is I just can't keep up with the demand. I'm just too old to keep a big farm of 'em. If I used inferior technique I probably could but then they wouldn't be so tasty. I've got my pride about them."

"Tasty," Kogan said. He looked thoughtful. Straightening his jacket, he took a breath. "People like your chickies that much?"

The farmer nodded. The chickies clucked in the background.

A look of determination came over Kogan's face. He nodded to himself and clapped the farmer on the back.

"Mr. Jenkins, I believe we can do some business."

The farmer grinned. "Mr. Kogan, you won't be sorry. These are the best little chickies in the county."

Rain started falling, in slow motion at first and then with gathering speed. The farmer and Kogan returned to look at the chickies. The chickies ran back and forth along the inside of the coop. The farmer pointed.

"See how strong they are? You'll have to tell your peoples to be careful around 'em," the farmer warned.

Kogan smiled. His face was still a little pale, but was returning to normal. "Don't worry, Mr. Jenkins. I'll explain everything to them. Mighty tasty."

One of the chickies pressed its face up to the fence. "Please, what's happening?" it asked. It tried to reach through the fence with grasping fingers.

The farmer chuckled. "Such lively little chickies. Come back to the house, Mr. Kogan, before you get too wet."

The two men turned and walked away from

the coop, as the storm, holding back no longer, began to sweep across the dark fields.

The farmer held the door for Kogan and looked out to watch the rain. Already the heat was diminishing. Overnight storm would do everything good, wash away all the dirt. It was one of the things that made his chickies so strong, leaving them out sometimes to deal with the elements. Made them strong and hardy. Good little chickies. Good eating.

Skin Deep

The day after the big presentation, he forgot his umbrella on the way to work and that's when he noticed them. He'd never noticed them before, had never looked up at precisely that angle in the five years he'd lived in the building. But there they were, staring down at him with stone gray eyes, a tiny hole in the centre to mark a pupil. Startled, he looked up at them for several minutes, the rain dripping off his hair like slimy sweat and down his neck onto his shirt. The chill that goose pimpled his neck wasn't from the rain. Grotesque, ugly faces grimaced down at him, stone wings spreading out in a horrible embrace. Gargoyles.

The rain made him blink, breaking the spell. Stone gargoyles, just part of the building. So what if he never noticed them before. He was only startled, that was all, not frightened. Besides, he was late for the office and now soaking wet. Turning up his collar, he ran down the steps, waving his briefcase at a passing taxi.

At the office, he was a celebrity.

"Good morning, Mr. Richards." The main receptionist smiled widely at him, something she'd never done before. Saving the Biscali account had definitely affected his standing.

"Morning." He snapped. Her gaze dropped away. Smarmy bitch. One cheery 'good morning' wasn't going to make him her ally.

He was hanging up his coat in his office when Leon Webster knocked and poked his head in.

"Busy, Doug?"

"No, just arrived."

Leon slipped in, closing the door behind him. His tall, gangly frame was swathed in an expensive, gray Armani suit. In two steps he covered the distance to the desk and sat down in one of the two green leather chairs in front of Doug's desk.

"Have a seat," Doug said wryly.

"That was a fantastic presentation," Leon said. "Everyone's talking about it. The way you smoothed things over when Steve started giving them an idea exactly like one they'd done three years ago, how you jumped in and said you'd discarded that option because Biscali was a forward thinking company." Leon shook his head. "Wonderful save. Almost as if you planned it." He paused and leaned forward. "Did you?"

Doug held up his hands. "Hey, I'm only the junior partner on this project. Steve preferred that we come up with separate ideas and he never told me what he was working on. You know how secretive and protective he became after the Williamson problems. I asked him to tell me where his thoughts were heading but he never did.

I thought for sure he knew about their previous campaigns." A shrug conveyed the inevitability of Steve's downfall.

Leon smiled. "Okay, have it your way. You don't have to tell me. But you should know that Henderson has been talking about you."

Doug brushed his hair back to cover his alarm. "What's he saying?" God, he hoped he sounded casual.

Leon smiled again, his teeth a tiny row along the edge of his thin lips. With his large nose, he looked like a shark eyeing a smaller fish. "He was impressed with your leadership abilities. I wouldn't be surprised if I smell a promotion."

Doug relaxed. Leon had a tendency to exaggerate somewhat, but he always knew the direction things were heading in. Maybe Henderson wasn't thinking of a promotion right now but he would be. Soon.

"I just did my job," Doug said.

"For the good of the company, that's heart-warming. Make sure you practice that enough so you can say it without laughing."

Doug grinned. "You think I haven't been?"

They both laughed. A knock interrupted them. Doug called out.

"Come in."

The door opened, casting a shadow across the carpeting that for a moment looked weirdly distorted, like some thin wings. An odd image, Doug thought and pushed it from his mind.

Steve Fesburger stood in the doorway. Although his dark blue suit was as neatly pressed as usual, it didn't stretch across his body the way it normally did. Fesburger appeared shrunken, like he had lost a lot of weight overnight.

"Can I speak to you, Doug?" he said quietly.

"I'll let you know about that item." Leon rose smoothly from his chair and crossed to the doorway.

"Good to see you, Steve," he said as he slipped out into the hallway. Fesburger turned to watch him go then entered the office and shut the door.

"The presentation went well," Doug said casually. "I hear Biscali is very pleased and wants to start on the first batch of commercials right away."

Fesburger smiled thinly. "Of course, they're pleased. They saw a first class snow job."

"Pardon?"

"You knew. You knew my ideas had already been done before." Fesburger leaned over the desk, casting a grey shadow across the desk blotter.

"How could I possibly know that when you didn't bother to tell me anything about what you were doing?" Doug spoke patiently. Why the hell should he play the bad guy to make a spineless jellyfish like Fesburger feel better? Just because he couldn't be bothered to do the proper research on the client. Sure, Doug had pulled all the files on Biscali's campaigns but Fesburger could have asked for them. Doug would have handed them over. Eventually. He picked up a pen from his desk and noticed the shadow.

The shape was odd, more defined than it should have been under the ambient light in the office. Normally Doug used the desk lamp but he hadn't had a chance to turn it on. Yet the shadow had a distinct shape, like a round swollen belly. Was that a snout on top? Fesburger's shoulders rising back from it, almost like wings.

"I don't remember you ever asking any questions about what I was doing."

Doug pulled his gaze away from the shadow.

Why did it unnerve him so? He focused on Fesburger's fleshy face.

"At least I took the time to do my homework."

Fesburger recoiled. The wrinkles around his mouth quivered.

"I got a kid in college and another in high school," he said softly.

Doug leaned back in his chair, steepled his fingers. "Yes, congratulations."

Fesburger's mouth opened, then clamped shut. Without another word, he turned and stalked out of the office, slamming the door behind him. Poor Fesburger, he'd forgotten how the game was played. Doug took a deep breath and let it out slowly. He didn't like such blatant confrontations. That was why his hands trembled. It had nothing to do with shadows.

On the way home from work, he reviewed his notes. The subway car rocked around him; people swayed in unison. On one of the pages, Doug noticed a doodle he'd done during Steve's part of the presentation. Strange. Usually he doodled golf clubs or cars. This one was a face, stark cheek-bones, thin lips pulled back from the sharp teeth. The eyes stared at him as if they were alive.

The subway jolted and the person next to him jostled his arm. Doug glanced up and then back at the paper.

The doodle had changed. The mouth opened wider revealing rows of needle-like teeth. Angry brows drew down over the piercing eyes.

Paper crinkled as Doug's fingers tightened on it. Doodles couldn't change like that, their ears couldn't get pointier, their expressions couldn't get nastier. Sweat prickled on Doug's back beneath his silk shirt. The paper trembled as his hands shook.

Of course, it hadn't changed, he told himself. It had originally looked like that.

He shoved the papers back into his briefcase.

Leaving the subway, he walked down the street, head down. He concentrated on the Biscali account. Forget the doodle.

He was being watched.

He stopped in the street, staring around. The feeling of eyes watching him was overwhelming but the only people on the street was a woman cooing over a stroller and an old man reading a paper at a bus stop. No one looked at him but he felt it on the back of his neck, prickling the hairs like static.

Slowly, he looked up. At the buildings.

They stared down at him. Faces of gray stone, scowling with open mouths. Clawed hands clutched at the air. He could almost feel them clutching at the fabric of his wool suit.

His mouth dried up. Even the ones that faced away from him looked at him out of the corner of their eyes. Jesus, that big one on the third floor on the right, did it move?

Clutching his briefcase, he ran for his own building at the end of the block.

He didn't look up as he jammed the key in the lock and turned it. The door opened with agonizing slowness. He raced for the elevator.

Only when his apartment door was safely shut behind him, did he let himself relax. The brief-case slipped from his fingers and landed on the foyer tile with a thud.

God, his heart was pounding and he needed a

drink. He moved to the bar and poured himself a shot of scotch. After gulping it, he poured another and moved to the window.

What the hell was the meaning of all the gargoyles? Probably nothing, just stress from work. Biscali was an important client. He didn't want to screw up. Now Fesburger he wanted to screw up, but not himself. This was his big opportunity to move forward. He'd spent years working for this, long hours in the office, sacrificed so much. Whole chunks of himself or at least Diane had claimed but what had she known? As he'd moved up she'd become less approving, constantly frowning, dragging him down. He didn't need that, didn't need her demands, her insistent on talking about their "relationship." Oh please. He'd finally had enough and said so to her voicemail. Then his mother had harped on him about that and his father complained about his career. They wanted him to do something positive and to give them grandchildren, like he owed it to them. But what it really boiled down to was that they wanted him to be as mediocre and pathetic as they were. When he'd had enough of their whining, he stopped taking their calls. He couldn't afford the distraction. Any distraction could mean failure.

His fingers tightened around the glass. He wouldn't fail. Turning his back on the window, he retrieved his briefcase. Inside were the presentation notes. Carefully, he avoided the piece of paper with the doodle as he settled down to do some work.

After several hours he knocked off. He'd completed a further breakdown of the campaign spots, fleshing out the concepts in detail. Tomorrow he'd run them by Henderson, being careful to copy Fesburger as well. That promotion would be coming but he had to make sure he didn't step on any obvious toes, even if those toes belonged to someone on the way down. Of course Fesburger didn't have to see it immediately. Late afternoon would suffice, say just after five. It wouldn't be Doug's fault if Fesburger didn't check his email in the evening.

A celebration was in order. He scrolled through his address list. Several possibilities, ah yes, there she was, Maureen. He picked up his cordless phone and dialed.

"Talk to me," she answered, making the words sound like a proposition.

"It's Doug."

"Doug darling, I was just on my way out," she purred. "I'm so glad I didn't miss your call."

"Where are you going?"

"Marshall is having a showing at a night club down on Richmond, a new place called Edges. Lots of drinks. Want to come?"

It wasn't exactly what he had in mind. A private celebration with her and her plastic sheets was more to his liking but he knew if he humoured her she'd be more than accommodating.

"Give me the address," he said.

The rain had returned while he'd been working. He stepped out of the cab and hunched his shoulders against it. The streets glistened like slime beneath the street lights. Wetness hung in the air like a fine mist even though the rain itself had stopped for the moment. The air smelled of rotting mold.

Maybe this wasn't such a good idea, Doug thought. The weather definitely dampened his mood and the look of the night club didn't improve it. The front was some kind of urban nightmare, all crumbling brick and ironwork sticking out haphazardly. Destined to be current for exactly one week before falling out of favour. A brilliant green neon sign advertised "Edges" in script. Even with the door closed he heard the thump of bass.

Something about the lines of the building disturbed him but before he could turn back, the cabby hit the gas and roared off into the darkness. Now he had to go inside. Either that or end up soaked.

The cover charge turned out to be an outrageous twenty-five dollars, mimed out by the cashier. It was impossible to hear over the raging noise. Doug paid and slipped in behind a couple wearing red velvet.

People jammed the room. Smoke hung like a false ceiling several feet above their heads. The bar was on the right, red velvet curtains lining the wall behind the bartenders, pierced randomly by the blades of various knives and swords.

At least he wasn't too out of place with his black pants and black t-shirt underneath his leather jacket. Squeezing through the crowd, he made his way to the bar where he spent five minutes yelling the word "scotch" at the bartender.

Finally the bartender nodded and stepped away. Doug allowed his gaze to wander over the various hilts sticking out of the wall. And this was supposed to be art. The closest hilt was old, the leather wrapping the handle cracked and weathered. A jewel glistened on the end, held in place by a carved creature with talons enclosing the jewel. A small head peered over the top, its face leering with a thin lipped smile, sharp cheeks and pointed ears. Impossibly, the head swiveled until the piercing eyes stared right at him. It winked.

A hand caressed his buttocks.

Doug jumped. His heart pounded in echo to the throbbing music. He whirled to find Maureen smiling. Leather straps crisscrossed her chest, barely containing her hefty breasts. Her blonde hair piled on her head shimmered in the dimness. Her thigh pressed against him, barely covered by a micro mini skirt.

When she saw his expression her smile faded. "What's wrong?" her mouth formed the words although he couldn't hear her.

He shook his head and leaned forward to kiss her. She'd startled him, that was all. Just startled. Sweat trickled down his spine.

The bartender returned with his drink. Doug paid and took a sip as the bartender moved away. It was rye.

After an hour, Doug managed to pry Maureen away from her friends and take her home. The sex was worth enduring the smoke and noise. Maureen thrived on it, her passion leaving him breathless. Finally she lay beside him, her eyes closed. Doug breathed in the sweet smell of her sweat and closed his eyes, allowing himself to start to fall asleep.

"Doug," her voice called.

"Umhmm," he mumbled.

"Did you like the show?"

"Umm."

"I thought it was quite breathtaking," she said. "Those swords especially, such detail. I really liked the jewel encrusted ones."

"Right, babe," he agreed and drifted away as she talked.

Cool air on his face woke him up. Darkness still filled the bedroom. Maureen lay curled up beside him, her blonde hair obscuring her face. A draft stirred several wisps as he watched. A draft? Where was that coming from? He was sure the window was closed. He looked over and thought he had to be asleep. Yes, asleep and dreaming. Stone gargoyles didn't tap at your window when you were awake.

He could see them through the white sheers, the mottled stone of massive shoulders, shifting grey as the light reflected off them. A hand lifted up, revealing three inch claws. They clicked on the window, tapping an irregular rhythm.

Was the window unlocked? He couldn't remember the last time he'd opened it, couldn't remember if he'd locked it afterward. His heart pounded. The claws tapped louder, more insistent. It was trying to get in, trying to get at him. He could already feel the coldness of its stone hands on his skin. Its chill would permeate his flesh all the way down to his bones, freezing him in place. His eyes stared at the window. The gargoyle's mouth opened, impossibly wide, revealing finely pointed teeth. As he watched, it stretched toward him, moving through the glass as if through fog. His mouth went dry, his throat tightened. He couldn't move or cry out. He was trapped by those piercing eyes, the gaping mouth.

The gargoyle paused above him, mouth open. Its breath smelled of moss and mildew, a thick, suffocating stench. It rested on his chest, pressing down so hard he could barely draw a breath. Claws shredded the blankets, plucking his skin underneath.

Beside him, Maureen sighed in her sleep.

The mouth moved forward again, toward his face, open, the stench overpowering. Unable to look away, unable to scream, his heart pounding heavily in his chest, Doug waited until he felt the sharp scrap of its teeth as it bit deeply into his cheek.

His shriek mixed with the screech of the alarm clock. He bolted upwards, struggling against the covers that wrapped around his legs. The alarm screamed until he hit the clock.

The bedroom door swung wide open.

"Doug, what is it?" Maureen, blonde hair sticking out, stood in the doorway.

He blinked stupidly at her. "Nothing," he said. "It's nothing. I have to get to work."

At the office, he stared out the window, distracted. The Biscali file sat on his desk but he wasn't interested in it. Right now his sanity interested him more.

Was he losing his mind? That was the only thing he could think of, the only reason he could come up with. Gargoyles were not out to get him. They weren't even alive. Just decorations made of stone and mortar.

Maybe it was stress. He'd been pushing hard the past few months, preparing for the presentation. Naturally he'd be feeling stressed and it was manifesting itself with this gargoyle obsession.

He took a deep breath and let it out slowly. As soon as this campaign was over he'd take a few days off. Maybe drive along the coast and find a little bed and breakfast or go up north and spend some time in a lodge deep in the woods. He'd take Maureen, if she could bear to be out of the city longer than twenty minutes. If not, he'd call up another of his women.

That started him thinking about the campaign. Henderson wanted to review the highlights at ten thirty. He glanced at his watch. Shit, it was twenty after.

Gathering up his papers, he stuck them in a file and left the office. He stopped in the washroom and splashed cold water onto his face. A haunted looking man with hollow eyes looked out at him from the mirror. What the hell was going on? A few days ago he was the bright star, now he looked like shit. His eyes narrowed as he glared at his image. He was not going to let this anxiety destroy him. He was stronger than this silliness. Afraid of gargoyles, ha!

Taking a deep breath, he picked up his notes and strolled to Henderson's office.

Leon Webster was already there, seated at the small conference table. Henderson rose, holding out a fleshy hand for Doug to shake. Steve Fesburger's absence spoke volumes.

"Come in, Doug, we're just getting ready to start," Henderson's deep voice rumbled.

Doug sat across from Leon and opened his file.

"I have to say again that your presentation to Biscali was top notch," Henderson said. "They were most impressed and so was I." He nodded meaningfully to Doug.

Doug acknowledged the nod with a smile.

"And," Henderson continued, "they were intrigued by your concept of using gargoyles to represent their pasta."

Doug's smile faltered. "Excuse me?"

"A wonderful symbol," Henderson said. "I liked how you described them as protectors and that Biscali pasta would be viewed as health conscious."

Doug stared at the old man. What the hell was he talking about? The presentation never mentioned gargoyles, the whole concept had centred around a fast-paced, urban lifestyle.

"I have to admit I think it also has an interesting quality," Leon said. He smiled broadly.

Doug pressed his palms to the table to prevent his hands from shaking. Was this some kind of joke? No, it couldn't be. Henderson would never do such a thing.

Carefully, he looked down at his notes, at the

presentation handouts. The top page was adorned with a stylized gargoyle.

He took the afternoon off and stopped at the liquor store on the way home. From there, he hunched in the back of a taxi, clutching a bottle of scotch. He sat in the centre of the backseat, away from the windows because they were looking for him. He could feel their questing gaze prickling his skin like the needles of a pine tree.

In his apartment, he locked the door and briefly considered pulling a chair in front of it. But that wasn't where they would come in. They'd come through the windows.

Taking the cordless phone and the scotch, he retreated to the bathroom, the only room without a window. After locking the door, he cracked open the bottle and took a long swallow.

Somehow they'd changed the presentation. He didn't understand how, but they'd done it. Gone was his entire idea of fitting into the urban lifestyle with exciting visuals and catchy music. In its place was the gargoyle idea of solidity and tradition.

He could almost stomach the idea if there hadn't been a underlying layer of malice to it. The illustrations seemed to almost jump off the page with a hyper reality that made Henderson's office feel fake. At one point as they reviewed the multimedia presentation, Doug could have sworn he caught a whiff of mold and decay drifting off the computer screen.

He swallowed another gulp of scotch. What could he do? How could he fight them? His trembling fingers jabbed at the phone and before he realized it, he'd punched in Maureen's number.

Maybe he could tell her. She was creative and imaginative, maybe she could help him make sense of what was happening. He held the phone to his ear and listened to it ringing.

Her answering machine clicked on and her voice flooded his ear with her familiar breathy tones. The beep sounded. He opened his mouth and realized he didn't know what to say. Hi babe, the gargoyles are after me. She would just laugh.

Even if he could fully explain his fear, he realized she wouldn't listen. Their relationship wasn't exactly based on mutual understanding, more often mutual lust. He barely tolerated her wild eccentricities while she tried not to be bored by his career. What did they really have in common?

Someone had to help him, but who could he ask? Leon was another hot dogger, eager to race up the ladder, content to share the rung until it got narrow enough for only one person. To Henderson he was the most recent boy wonder and was only interesting as long as he performed. Fesburger would never speak to him again but was that his fault? He hadn't exactly ruined the guy's career even if he hadn't helped it.

Why was this happening? He'd always taken great pains to control his life on his terms. When his parents had expressed disappointment in his career choice, he'd cut them off and gone it alone. He didn't need their support, just like he didn't need Diane after she'd become too demanding. Marriage and children wasn't for him. That's why he preferred Maureen. No nasty entanglements.

He'd always been strong and hard. He'd had to fight to get what he wanted and he was willing to pay the price. No one else understood. Now these stone statues threatened to undo everything.

The bathroom lights made him squint. He swallowed more scotch. God, the bottle was half gone already. He should have bought more. He started to raise the bottle to his lips.

What was he doing? Drink anymore and he'd fall asleep. Then they'd get him. He wouldn't be able to defend himself. He smashed the bottle into the sink, watching the amber fluid drain away. His trembling fingers clutched the phone in his lap.

He sat that way for countless hours, staring at the door. The fever of the alcohol bled out of him, leaving him twitchy. The bland fluorescent light made his eyes ache. He blinked.

And sat bolt upright. God, he'd been asleep. He stared wildly around the bathroom but it was empty, even the bathtub.

Something scratched at the door.

A light scratch, like a puppy. The phone clattered to the floor as Doug stood and pressed himself against the wall.

Another scratch, more insistent. The door rattled on its hinges. A crack appeared near the top. Doug opened his mouth to scream.

The door bowed inward and they came in through the cracks, three of them. The smell of mortar and cement drifted toward him, dust tickling his nose, making him want to sneeze. The one on the left, large wings folded behind its back, stepped forward on taloned feet. Beside it, a thin one stood almost shaped like a girl but the face was too long, the mouth pulled back in a sneer. Finally the third one he recognized from the night club. It had been wrapped around a jewel encrusted sword.

They lunged forward, grabbing him in an iron grip. Stone hands dragged him to the floor, freezing his skin. Doug struggled feebly, fear clutching his bowels but he couldn't break their grip.

He felt the tiny one scrabbling up his pant leg. It appeared on his chest and grinned at him, needle teeth gleaming in the light.

"Time," it squealed. "You're hard enough now."

Doug shook his head wildly, his eyes widening as the tiny face leaned forward.

"No," he moaned. The stench of decay almost made him gag.

The little gargoyle grabbed Doug's head and bent over to sink its teeth into his cheek.

Doug screamed, feeling his flesh tear away. A warm gush of blood spilled onto his chest. The little gargoyle spat out the skin and took another bite, digging down until it reached stone.

Satisfied it lifted its head and nodded to the others. Methodically, they dug their claws in and pulled. Skin peeled away, then muscle, revealing the grey mottled surface of stone. Finally they finished stripped the dripping layers away and stepped back to watch the first feeble movements. New talons, freshly revealed, scrapped at the tile as the new gargoyle tried to stand.

The others waited patiently. They didn't mind waiting, their waiting lasted years and they had been calling this one for a long time. Finally he had become hard enough to hear them. They watched with unblinking stone eyes as the new gargoyle lifted his face to them, realization flashing across his hard, cold features.

Time to go home.

FILE UNDER OBLIVION

After a week working in the file room Patty felt as if she'd been swallowed. The days became endless stretches of time she spent staring at files. The filing room was the last room on the floor, down a long gray hallway, after the cubicles, which held the final vestiges of life in the department. Inside, the cabinets were laid out in a grid, four rows, arranged by sections in alphabetical order, cross referenced numerically. Each file had a document list, but the lists needed updating and then she had to archive everything beyond three years old, as per schedule B, a mammoth schedule in the filing binder that the supervisor, Susan, had dumped into her hands on the first day. The binder had been so heavy Patty had almost dropped it on her foot, a fate that certainly would have sent her to the hospital and finished her chances at this assignment, however unglorious.

Yet here she was, staring at the procedures, learning that if the questioned document had to be archived, as instructed in the popular schedule B, she struck it from the file list and added it to the archive list.

Whatever happened to the paperless office, she wondered.

As she worked, boxes began to accumulate in the rows between filing cabinets. Soon she had to squeeze past them. Her sense of being cut off from the rest of the office increased. Was it possible that there was no office outside the file room? Maybe she was the only person on the floor. She tried to get to the coffee room at least once a day but she still didn't know anyone but Susan and only saw her irregularly. The file room became another dimension. With no windows, she couldn't see anything but the steel gray cabinets, open drawers gaping. When she stepped in through the doorway, the outside world ceased to exist.

Time stretched endlessly. Normally in a temp job this helped the job go quickly but she couldn't remember how long she'd been here. Two weeks? A month? No, that couldn't be right, the job only lasted a month. She lost track of the days and found herself sitting bewildered in her apartment on the weekend. On Monday, she returned to be shut up again in the steadily shrinking rows.

The fluorescent lights dried out her eyes and gave her headaches. The constant bending over and hefting of boxes made her back ache. Her hands, normally soft and well manicured, became rough and covered with paper cuts. Her nails chipped and broke as she pulled open the file drawers.

An endless stream of typed pages passed before her eyes, blurring into nonsense. Several times a day she found herself staring into space, holding a file she couldn't remember picking up.

Halfway through the second week she developed a headache that lingered no matter how many pain killers she took.

On the Friday afternoon of the second week Susan knocked on the file room door and poked her head in.

"Hey, this is terrific. You're doing a fantastic job."

Patty blinked. The headache arched across her brow as she lifted her head, making her wince.

"Thank you," she whispered.

Susan stepped in all the way, her hands planted on the hips of her smart navy suit. She nodded appreciatively at the stacks of boxes and piles of sorted files. Standing against the uniform gray of the cabinets, she looked hyper-real like a three-dimensional hologram from one of those cheesy science fiction movies from the fifties.

"This is definitely better," Susan said.

Patty clenched a file to her chest defensively. This woman's voice boomed and echoed through the file rows. Patty wasn't used to hearing voices anymore. She'd grown accustomed to the hum of the fluorescents and the whisper of the paper. Susan's words roared in her ears.

"We may have to extend your assignment," Susan said. "They're consolidating us with another department and we'll have to incorporate their files. They won't be arriving for another two months but I'm sure we can get another three months of work for you. Is that all right?"

"Fine," Patty mumbled. Anything to make her leave, anything to regain the silence.

"Great, I'll have Monica call your agency." With a dazzling smile that made Patty squint, Susan left.

That evening, Patty microwaved a TV dinner and stood mechanically chewing in the kitchen. Her fridge was almost bare but she had no energy for shopping. No energy even for cooking which was something she loved to do. It had always relaxed her. But since she'd started this job it was all she could do not to go to bed by eight.

The phone rang, startling her. She turned to stare at it like it was some alien contraption. After a moment, she put down her Salisbury steak and answered it.

"Hello?"

"Patty, where are you?"

The question confused her and it took her a moment to recognize Lucy's voice.

"I'm here," she answered.

"I know you are but you're supposed to be here," Lucy said, exasperation clear in her voice.

Patty tried to think. Was she supposed to be doing something tonight?

"Sorry, I don't remember."

"You forgot to write it down, didn't you?" Lucy scolded. "We're at Toby's. It's Janet's birthday. Remember we're going out for dinner and dancing."

A vague memory of the conversation filtered into her mind but she couldn't focus on it. Dinner and dancing. That would mean she'd have to get dressed and go now. That would mean she'd have to move.

"I'm sorry, Lucy, I just don't think I can make it. This job has wiped me out and I think I'm coming down with something. I wouldn't want to infect Janet."

"Well." Patty could hear the indecision in Lucy's voice. She wasn't pleased that Patty was backing out but couldn't berate her for not exposing Janet to illness.

"Please give Janet my best and tell her I'll call her next week."

"Okay," Lucy said reluctantly. "Make sure you get lots of sleep." The comment sounded like a threat.

"I will." Patty hung up the phone.

The TV dinner was no longer appetizing and she dumped it into the garbage. In the living room she sat on the couch and stared at the blank television. What the hell was the matter with her? She never missed the opportunity to see her friends, especially Lucy and Janet whom she'd roomed with in college. But she couldn't even drum up any guilt. She couldn't raise up any emotion. This job was sucking the life from her. She'd never been so exhausted, so lethargic because of a placement before. Another three months of this, she thought. Could she survive it?

Of course, she could. It was just monotonous. She would get used to it, was already getting use to it. It had only been a couple of weeks, after all. Once she got farther into it she would get her energy back, get enthusiastic about finishing it and seeing the files all cleaned out. That would give her satisfaction. A job well done.

She smiled to herself and pretended she didn't feel any fear.

On Monday she took the subway to work and returned to the filing room.

The rows of cabinets seemed less bright to her today, as though the grey paint had dulled on the weekend. Files stuck together in the cabinet and she had to yank hard to release them. Her headache beat in her temples and thudded down her neck. She acquired three nasty paper cuts on her left hand before noon. She retreated to the staff kitchen to find the bandages. As she ripped the package open and wrapped her cuts, she suddenly realized the files had missed her.

She'd been gone an entire weekend and they'd missed her. Missed her touching them and sorting them and putting them away. When she returned to the filing room, she handled them more gently and the files responded. They lifted from the drawers with ease. Papers flew apart from each other. The boxes felt lighter.

She didn't get another paper cut that entire day.

No one had ever cared about them, she thought on the way home. No one had ever taken responsibility to make sure they were clean. It was always the last job on the list, more often forgotten than not. No wonder they were resentful.

She wouldn't forget. She would make sure they got sorted and cleared out. She would make them perfect.

Days and weeks flew by. Her energy came back, just like she'd predicted but only during the day when she was in the filing room. Then she filed and sorted and purged like a mad woman.

At home she slumped on her couch, ignoring the phone when it rang. Finally it stopped ringing. The silence soothed her. It was so noisy during the day, the files made such noise. Paper crackling and crumbling, boxes thudding, drawers sliding. They chattered at her, finally happy to have attention lavished on them. But the constant noise made her headache worse, so she sat at home alone in the stillness.

Besides, no one would really understand and she wasn't going to try to explain it. It was personal, a relationship between her and the files.

They were more than paper, more than words. They were ideas, forgotten ideas that needed to be recognized and respected. She understood that desire, being a temp, thrust into jobs where she was viewed as an extension of the furniture. She too needed recognition, if only from the way the files slowly became organized.

But as the days wore on it became evident that she wasn't up to the task.

She felt exhausted all the time even though she'd started going to bed by seven. She never took any breaks and ate her lunch propped up against the file boxes. She gave every ounce of energy she had, but it wasn't enough.

Soon the files looked sloppy again. Paper corners curled and the drawers stuck together. Moving the boxes became impossible. The other department's files were expected next week and her burden would triple. Just thinking about it made her knees wobble. She had to do something. She could feel the paper all around her, expectant. She wasn't enough anymore, but she had taken on the responsibility. What was she going to do about this?

The headache pounded in her temples. Panic made her heart pound in sympathy. What was she going to do?

By the time she made it to Susan's cubicle, she was out of breath.

Susan, looking calm and efficient in a gray suit, pulled a chair over and sat her down.

"Take it easy, Patty, catch your breath."

She sagged in the chair, gulping air. The long walk down the hallway had tired her out. Maybe she had that chronic fatigue disease. But no, that wasn't it. It was the files.

"Is something wrong?" Susan asked.

"The files," Patty said. "I need some help."

"I'm not surprised," Susan said. "Actually, I've been meaning to tell you. Everyone is thrilled with the job you're doing. It hasn't gone unnoticed."

Normally such praise would have made Patty beam and spread a warm glow of pride through her. But now her own petty pride was unimportant. The files were getting messy and she hadn't the strength to keep up.

"When are the new department files due?" she asked.

"In another week. We were going to hire someone to help you with them."

"Could they start sooner?" Patty asked. God, she hoped she didn't sound too desperate.

Susan smiled. "Don't worry about it. We'll get someone tomorrow."

Relief flooded Patty. Quickly she took her leave from Susan and retreated back to the filing room. Inside, she walked up and down the rows, touching a drawer, running her finger tips over the plastic tabs, stroking the labels.

"Someone is coming," she whispered to them. "Someone is coming tomorrow."

She got to work early the next day to prepare. From the supply cabinet she pulled a new box of file folders, a roll of labels and a stack of plastic tabs. She reviewed the inventory arranged neatly on a file box. Around her she could feel the files almost vibrating with anticipation. Soon now, soon. She was almost as excited as the files were. Her skin tingled. Her ever-present headache loosened on her neck.

At nine o'clock Susan knocked on the file room door and entered, leading a tall, slender woman. She wore a conservative, navy suit with her blonde hair pulled back into a bun.

Patty fixed a smile onto her face, trying not to giggle. She could feel the files all around them, attention riveted. She would have to do this right.

"Patty, this is Muriel," Susan said. "She's here to help you get ready for the file merging and complete it."

"It's nice to meet you," Patty said eagerly. She thrust her hand toward the blonde woman.

Muriel's smile was a little nervous. "I hope I can help."

"Oh I think you will." Patty nodded.

"I'll leave you to it," Susan said. "Patty's been working with the files for a month now and knows more about it than I do."

She chuckled and left. The sound of her heels echoed down the hall.

"I'll show you the manual first," Patty said. She dug under a stack of files and pulled out the binder.

"These are the codes and we use schedule B for the archiving."

She handed the binder to Muriel who took it with a look of surprise. Just like me when I first got here, Patty thought. Had it only been a month ago? It felt more like a lifetime.

Muriel bent over the binder, bewilderment crossing her face. The pages turned crisply beneath her fingers. Patty stood watching, her back against a filing cabinet. She could feel the handle pressing against her buttocks. Her fingers tingled from the touch of the binder.

Would she understand? Patty wondered. Her heart began to pound. She swallowed extra saliva in her mouth. Would the files accept Muriel as they had her? She could almost hear them rustling expectantly. They too were eager for fresh hands, fresh devotion. Could Muriel be the one?

"This is very detailed," Muriel said.

"Don't worry, I'll help you," Patty said. "Let's start with the simple stuff first."

By noon, Muriel had removed her jacket and rolled up the sleeves of her blouse. Several blonde strands had pulled free from her bun and hung like shredded tissue paper around her face. Although she moved efficiently and seemed to be learning the system, she didn't look as though she was connecting. Patty frowned in disappointment. Muriel didn't care anything at all about the files. She simply wanted to get the job done.

"Ow, dammit." Muriel sucked her baby finger. She glanced over at Patty. "I hate paper cuts."

Patty forced a sympathetic smile onto her face. Even the files knew.

"Let's break for lunch," Patty said. "I think we'll have to work late tonight. I hate to do this to you on your first day, but with the other department's files arriving in a week we don't have a lot of time."

Muriel sighed. "That's okay. It's extra money, right?"

Patty smiled. "Extra money. Right."

She felt the files waiting around her all afternoon and it made her edgy. She wasn't sure exactly what they wanted her to do. It was apparent that Muriel was unsuitable to them. The disappointment made her sluggish and she responded slowly to Muriel's questions. She had been so hopeful this morning. At least then she could imagine there would be a brief respite from the files' relentless demands. Now there was no hope. She was alone again.

They worked past five o'clock without noticing. Finally at a quarter to six, Patty felt the files stirring. The whisper of the paper reached her ears. She glanced over at Muriel who was busy pasting labels on new folders. She hadn't heard anything. The files were being careful.

Slowly, Patty wandered toward the door. It was kept open to allow for ventilation. She closed it softly. With the door closed, the room was virtually isolated at the end of the hall. No one would hear anything.

The rustling got louder. Cautiously, Patty peered around the corner of the one of the file cabinets. Muriel was finally noticing something. She had looked up from her labels, her head turning around to look at the cabinets.

Several papers hiding on top of the cabinet near Muriel's head came fluttering down like monstrous snowflakes. Muriel looked up and one of the papers flew by her cheek, its edge slicing her flesh.

She jumped to her feet, scattering the files on her lap. Her hand went up to her face and came away bloody.

"Shit," she snapped. She looked up as Patty stepped into view. "Look at this. The vent must have blown them off the cabinet."

"Must have," Patty agreed. She took another step. The files rustled, urging her on. Her hands were dry, almost cold. They itched to touch paper.

"Damn, I'm dripping on my blouse." Muriel began to move past Patty. "I'll just go to the washroom."

Patty lunged sideways, knocking Muriel over. She fell in an avalanche of paper. Her hands and feet scrambled for purchase, but the files slipped and slid under her touch.

"Why the hell did you do that?" Muriel snapped, struggling to stand.

"You don't understand," Patty said. "You don't appreciate them. They don't like it."

She picked up a stack of files and flung them in Muriel's face. "Neither do I."

Muriel's mouth opened. Patty didn't hear any sound. Paper leapt at Muriel's face, stuffing into her mouth, gagging her. On and on they lunged from Patty's hand, pushing into Muriel's mouth, forcing down her throat. Soon Muriel's struggles slowed and then ceased. Her face disappeared beneath a stack of monthly reports.

Patty stepped back. She was breathing hard and sweat trickled down her back. Her arms ached and her fingers tingled. But she hadn't done anything.

The files. They had done it.

Now she would have to clean up.

It was easier than she expected. Muriel folded nicely into one of the extra large filing boxes. Patty covered her with old spreadsheets and used the trolley to wheel her out of the filing room. She took the elevator down to the basement and dumped the box into the industrial shredder container. According to the monthly scheduled, it was due to be emptied tomorrow and taken to the processing plant for automatic disposal. No one actually looked in the container once it was filled.

By the time she got home it was almost midnight, but instead of feeling exhausted, she felt liberated. The files had looked the cleanest they had ever looked since she'd started. Everything left was pristine. The hangers hung straight and clean. The drawers opened and closed soundlessly.

They'd been hungry, she realized. She'd given all the devotion they needed, but they'd wanted something else. Her reflection in the bathroom mirror smiled back, shadows forking beneath her eyes and down her cheeks. They'd been hungry and now they were fed.

"I haven't seen Muriel today," Susan said to Patty as they stood at the coffee maker. "Is she coming in later?"

"I don't know," Patty said. "I don't think she really liked this job. Actually, I'd be surprised if she showed up again."

Susan sighed, stirring cream into her coffee. "I really wish people would let me know before they just decide to pick up and leave. I guess it's the hazards of hiring temps. Oh, no offence, Patty."

Patty smiled a radiant grin that lit up her entire face. "None taken, Susan. But while we're on the subject, I think I'm going to need more help in the file room. You know with the new department files coming soon. There will be so many more files and they'll definitely need tending to."

"Don't you worry, Patty. I'll make sure we find someone. Maybe even a couple of people. And I want you to know that we're going to need you to stay on for another six months or so, just to make sure everything is running smoothly. Who knows what might even happen after that?"

Patty nodded, stirring her own coffee. "Six months will be fine. I'm sure with a couple more bodies, the files will be finished in no time."

WILD CALL

During the long hours of summer sunshine Buck searched for gold. His sled dogs, so thin when they finally managed to get to Stewart in the late spring, now romped among the brittle summer grass. When he called them in to eat, he admired the return of the healthy sheen of their coats. Muscles, once stringy from the hardships of winter, drew firm and strong again. When he was finished with them, he knew he'd get a good price for them in Dawson.

Meanwhile, he spent his day working the river as he waited for his partner Henry to return with more provisions. Henry had taken their second dog team to sell. He would then return on his own with some promised luxuries.

The search for gold was slow and back breaking, but Buck didn't mind. The sun warmed his face. The fresh scent of wild flowers and grass rode the breeze. In the evenings he stretched out beside the small crumbling log cabin Henry had found to watch the sun slowly moving across the sky. It felt odd to have the sun shining down so late at night. Often he'd shake himself to find it was almost midnight and well time he got to sleep. Strange to sleep when the sun still shone, but he knew as the summer waned, the cold darkness would return, slowly creeping to claim the frozen heart of this northern land.

He wanted to be gone before that happened, back to the bustle of San Diego where Sadie waited. She was patient but her father was not. He could all but see the old man's disapproving face in Sadie's last letter. If he and Henry managed to hit a large strike, that old man's disapproval would vanish. No, not if. When. It would happen.

He worked the river extra hard that afternoon.

The dogs barking finally reminded him to feed them. He was surprised to find it was after eight. The dogs trailed him back to the cabin, dancing on frantic legs until he tossed a fish to each of them. He and Henry had agreed to continue the food rationing. Now that they were settled, the dogs could hunt for extra food if they wanted it. It gave them good exercise and kept them sharp.

After feeding the dogs, he fed himself but it was mostly by rout. He didn't taste any of the mush. Instead he stared at the sky, watching the sun in the seemingly eternal bright sky.

That evening he went to bed early and put a strip of cloth over his eyes to block the sunlight. Already he could feel the nights becoming cooler although it was still only the beginning of September. They had a huge stash of wood by the side of the cabin but he should collect more scrub and twigs for kindling. He'd start that in the morning. Planning his day, he fell asleep...

And woke to howling.

The darkness disoriented him. He'd forgotten what it was like, so used to the sun. For a moment, he was back in San Diego, in the filthy room off the alley and the howl was a fight outside. Then he remembered. The Yukon, and the howl was a wolf.

The dogs were snarling, crying out. Buck stumbled out of bed, grabbing for the rifle. The darkness tripped him up, hid the rifle, then reluctantly released it as Buck's eyes adjusted. By the time he threw the door open, he could see.

He fired a shot into the sky. Most times, the noise scared a pack off. The dogs yelped, rushed the cabin. Buck pushed through, waving the rifle, yelling. He couldn't see the wolf pack, just that incessant howling. It sounded like it came from everywhere.

His foot slipped and he fell. The rifle jolted from his hand, landed a few feet away. He scrabbled for it and stopped, seeing a thin wolf-like shadow. It pounced on top of one of the smaller dogs, Slade. Slade yowled, shoulder torn open to the bone. The dog staggered, fell. The wolf, all bone and snarl, jumped forward, slashing open Slade's throat then bounced away. Buck watched, hypnotized as the dog's jerking body spasmed one final time and lay still.

Then he felt the wolf eyes turn to him, staring. That cold, harsh glare sized him up, measuring the distance to strike. The rifle was between him and the wolf. A few feet. Could have been a few miles, a few hours. The wolf head dipped. One paw stepped forward. No howling now. Even the dogs behind him were quiet. Expectant. Only a few feet.

He dove for the gun as the wolf leapt. Now it snarled, a loud roar. He felt its breath on his face, hot and wet. Its spit dotted his face. No time for aiming. He pulled the trigger. The roar of the gun undercut his own shriek of pain as claws tore his left shoulder.

The wolf fell away. No triumphant leap aside. It landed in a heap, moaning. Buck dragged himself back. Let the dogs finish it. His shoulder ached where the wolf had slashed him. Using the rifle as a crutch, he pulled himself to his feet and staggered back toward the cabin. The dogs moved forward, dark shadows. He heard them growling as he shut the cabin door.

He lit a lamp to see that his left shoulder was worse than he'd thought. Blood streamed down his arm and soaked his pants. He used his sleeping cloth dunked in water to wipe the worst of it away. The slashes were deep, difficult for him to tend to alone. He pulled out his only clean shirt and used it to bind his shoulder. He tied it with rope, as tight as he could, his breathing hissing out with the pain. Henry was due back any day now. Would probably come walking back into the camp tomorrow and he would know what to do. Henry was always on about healing potions, he would have something to help for sure.

Buck concentrated on that, pushing any fear far back into his mind. He didn't have to worry now. The wolf was dead. The dogs had finished it off; he still heard them snarling outside. Sleep began to overtake him even as he sat down on the bed. He allowed it to pull him down, obliterating the final, lingering question in his mind.

Wolves hunted in packs. So where was the pack?

In the morning, his shoulder had stiffened and he could barely get out of bed. Finally he rolled onto his right side and pushed himself up. The dull ache told him he had at least survived the night.

Outside, the thought of food made his stomach churn but he forced himself to drink water. A patch of damp ground was the only trace left of the wolf. Buck sat down to rest after the effort of leaving the cabin. So much for working the river today.

Despite the sunshine, the air was chilled and Buck knew the summer was ending. Already he could tell the sun was not as powerful as before. Here at the top end of the world, day and night battled savagely for dominion. The reign of day was slowly coming to an end and night would soon be supreme.

Buck did not want to be around for that but his wounded shoulder threatened his plans. With Henry slow to return, the envisioned strike before winter dimmed. They might have to struggle through another six months which meant hanging on to the dogs and fighting to survive here. He knew he could do it, had done it, but wanted to be gone. He'd had enough of this land. He wanted a soft bed to sleep in, wanted to wake up to a hot fresh meal and see Sadie's smile. He pushed the thoughts away. No use dwelling. If Henry arrived soon then they might just make it back.

The sun inched across the sky and his shoulder ached. He kept thinking he should eat something but couldn't bring himself to do it. Once he bit off a mouthful of dried venison only to heave it back up. The only thing he could keep down was water and only that in little sips.

He spent the day watching the sun and the dogs. They romped around the cabin, pausing occasionally to look at him curiously. Usually he went down to the river and they were confused by the disrupted routine. Several times they came up to him to be fed but he shooed them away.

Henry didn't return that day, so Buck finally fed the dogs then retired to the cabin early. He sipped more water and again thought about food but couldn't muster enthusiasm for it. He lay down on the piled blankets. The sun still filtered through the slats of the cabin so he again placed the cloth strip across his eyes. Even as his hand fell back, he was asleep.

He dreamed of the forest, of moving through the trees in the darkness. The air was crisp and cold, the ground crunched beneath his feet. Up ahead he could smell prey, food, waiting for him to catch it. He heard the call, felt the vibration of it in his bones and it filled him with a desire stronger than he had ever known. Eagerly he moved through the woods, wanting to rush but knowing that loud noise would flush out the prey too quickly. But even as he thought it, he felt the prey move farther away and he gave chase.

Cold air filled his lungs as he ran through the forest. The wind howled around him, carrying him forward. He shouted out his own answer, his own excitement as he ran and it came echoing back through the trees. He knew he would catch the prey, knew he was gaining by each step. The trees flashed by. He pushed himself forward, felt his heart pounding, his blood warming him even in the freezing air. He shouted his imminent triumph to the wind and it howled back. The ground sloped and curved. The trees gave way to a small clearing and he could almost see his prey...

The dogs barking woke him. The morning had come awfully suddenly. Buck's shoulder throbbed as he pushed himself up and staggered out of the cabin. The dogs impatiently danced around, darting forward and back. What was the matter with them? He'd just fed them last night. He glanced into the sky and stopped.

The sun. It was in the wrong place. Had the world suddenly reversed it rotation? It should be rising.

He'd slept the entire day. Numbly, he tossed fish to the dogs then sat down on the log outside the cabin. How could he have slept the entire day? The wound had made him sleepy that he was sure of, but he'd never heard of a man having to sleep the entire day. He must have needed it. That much was obvious. Perhaps it would heal faster and he could get back to working the river again. Maybe by the time Henry returned, he would almost be back to normal.

Again he tried to eat and although he was hungry, he couldn't keep the food down. It tasted odd to him so he spat it out. Instead he continued to sip water as he sat up and watched the sun.

After a few hours he was tired. He dragged himself back into the cabin and noticed that the sun was lower than the night before. Full darkness was advancing on a daily basis now.

His dream took him back to the forest. He could see the trees more easily now and they looked different from the ones he knew. These were immensely old, suggesting a different time, a more ancient time. In this forest, no man had ever walked before. The howls he heard were from some long extinct beast. Hearing it stirred his blood, made his heart beat faster. It was the call of prey, the call to hunt and feed. He took off through the forest, chasing the howl.

The next day he again woke too late to do any work at the river. He fed the dogs and sat in front of the cabin, watching the sun, waiting. The throb of his shoulder was duller now and he removed the bloodied shirt to look at the wound. Crusted blood sealed it shut. He wrapped a rag soaked in water over the sight, wincing at the slight pain. As far as he could tell there was no infection. It would heal, leaving him with a long scar. It would probably ache when it rained, he thought. He considered food but it held no interest for him. He kept sipping water.

That night he stayed up, not tired. All the sleep he'd had left him restless but he couldn't work the river, didn't want to do it. He paced back and forth along the length of the cabin, five steps one way, four steps the other. The space was small and felt smaller by the second. Finally he left to stand outside.

The sun was almost down and darkness was creeping forward. Around him, the dogs were curled up asleep. Several twitched as they romped in their dreams. Buck walked over to the fire pit and kicked at the ash pile. He was hungry. He should start up a fire and cook something. He felt like he could gorge himself tonight. This was a good sign; his shoulder must be healing if his appetite had returned. He began to gather kindling to build a fire, but even as he lit it and nurtured the fire, his interest in food waned.

He didn't want to cook. He tried to think of all the meals he could have back in San Diego; thick, juicy steaks and large baked potatoes. Steaming lobster with fresh vegetables. The memories did nothing for him. He stamped the fire out and stirred the ashes. Best not to waste wood or kindling on a fire he wouldn't use.

Might as well go back to sleep, he thought, but he didn't want to. Around him, the trees blended into the darkness and instead of being as menacing as before, they seemed to invite him. He felt a stirring to go walk among them. Hadn't he dreamt of trees? He couldn't remember. Something about running, a howl calling him forward. It was dangerous to leave the cabin at night. The wolf attack several nights ago underlined the danger that lurked in that darkness but still he felt drawn forward. The urge to run made the muscles in his legs twitch. He stepped closer, watching the trees spread their branches open in welcome.

The skin in his shoulder itched as a cold breeze blew over him. He could almost hear something in the wind, a hint of prey and it stirred him. He moved faster into the trees. The crunch of the ground beneath his feet was loud. He could suddenly hear everything in the forest. The sway of the branches over his head, the rustle of the brush, the scurrying feet of some nearby animal. He paused, listening harder for it. Off to his left. He turned to follow.

The scurrying sounded louder as he drew near. Crouching, he peeked over a bush and saw a rabbit digging at the hard ground. It froze, then lifted its head, ears wide and listening. Buck held his breath. After a moment, the rabbit bent back to its task, scratching at the ground with its paws. Buck crouched lower, gathering his strength for one quick rush. He waited another moment, listening to the rabbit scrape. He shot forward.

Outreached hands missed the rabbit by inches. Startled, it leapt away and ran. Buck raced after it. The cold air stabbed his lungs, blasted his shoulder. He gulped air, felt his blood boil as he ran. Running through the forest he felt completely free. Each footfall was sure. He didn't worry about stumbling. He leapt through the trees as if he knew the way. He felt fully alive, fully aware of the prey racing away from him. He knew he would catch it, could almost feel his teeth sinking into the soft flesh, taste the rush of blood into his stomach, filling it, filling him. He would gorge in it, revel in his kill and howl his pleasure to the night sky.

Around a grove of trees, he saw the rabbit scurrying across a small clearing. He charged after it, narrowing the space. In the darkness, its fur looked silver, reflecting ambient light. He focused on the straining haunches and leapt forward.

His hand grabbed a leg and he held on. The rabbit screamed, scrambling to escape. Buck dragged it back and with a billow of triumph, sank his teeth into the rabbit's throat. It shrieked, the sound vibrating in his mouth as he chewed. He felt the body jerk and grow still. His hunger enveloped him and he tore savagely at the carcass.

As he licked the blood from his nails, a howl rose around him and he lifted his face to the sky, not aware that his mouth was open and his voice joining the call.

The sun made Buck blink. Had he left the cabin door open to let the strong sun shine through? He opened his eyes.

Trees surrounded him. He bolted up. Where was he? His hands were dirty with dried blood. Around him, bones and fur littered the ground. He stared at it, uncomprehending. Then memories came slowly back. The rabbit. The chase. The capture. His stomach lurched. He'd eaten the thing live.

It was hunger, he told himself, only hunger. After three days of course he'd been starved and acted like a madman. Who wouldn't? He stumbled back toward the cabin. He felt stronger now, better. He could return to working the river and wait for Henry. Then when Henry arrived, they could leave for good. He no longer cared if they found a rich strike of gold.

Through the day he forced himself to work the river, to return to his regular routine. But when it came time to feed the dogs, they wouldn't come near him, wouldn't take the fish he offered. He tossed it toward them but they whined at him and backed away. He shouted at them impatiently and one of them snarled. The sound enraged him and he leapt at the dog. His hands grabbed the muzzle and a front leg. Startled, the other dogs fled. The one in his hands tried to pull away. He snarled and sank his teeth into its fleshy throat.

Blood gushed into his mouth, igniting euphoria. It blazed within him as surely as the night overtook the day. All thoughts of leaving disappeared the same way the sun sank beneath the distant horizon. Soon the night spread across the land and Buck moved out into the forest to hunt the rest of the dogs down.

Two days later as the sun set early in the afternoon, Henry arrived at the camp. With a grunt, he dumped the pack off his back and dropped the lead of the small sled he'd been dragging. The camp was quiet and he thought that maybe Buck was down by the river working. He stowed the pack in the cabin and stepped outside, stretching his arms.

"Hey, Buck," he called. "You at the river? Where are the dogs?"

Silence answered him. It seemed odd that not one of the dogs had come at the sound of his voice to investigate. He glanced around and slowly noticed the small signs of disuse. The fire pit held a bare scattering of ashes. Bones littered the ground. He looked back at the cabin and remembered how the door had been open when he arrived.

Henry went to retrieve the rifle from his pack in the cabin. Inside, he noticed the disarray of the cabin. Buck had always been meticulous in his neatness. Packed a sled up neat, kept the cabin neat, because you might need something in a hurry and it should be where you need it. But now the cabin was a mess. The few pieces of clothing not tore into shreds were strewn across the floor. A single bottle of scotch lay in the centre, its liquid long drained away.

Something had happened. Indians maybe, Henry thought, but he'd never seen anything like this. Quickly, he loaded the rifle. By the time he left the cabin the sun was already down, leaving a last few streaks of orange across the cold, clear sky.

Damn, he couldn't go looking in the forest now. He set the rifle down against the cabin and gathered kindling to make a fire. A healthy pile of brush and twigs caught easily and soon he had a good blaze going. From the trees, he heard a twig snap, or was it from the fire? He peered out into the darkness but the brightness of the fire made it difficult to see. Was something out there? Maybe one of the dogs. If that were so, it would come to the fire, so maybe it was a wolf.

Henry reached for the rifle lying against the cabin wall.

Something howled and knocked him sideways. The rifle fell out of reach. He twisted away, toward the fire. The creature snarled in anger and darted back. Henry grabbed for the rifle, but the creature lunged forward, kicking it away.

Claws dug into his chest, shredding skin. Henry gasped in air, struggled to hit back. He stared up at the thing attacking him. Was it a wolf? No, it couldn't be. Not the way it held him down. Then he saw. A face, oh god, it was a face!

"Buck," he cried. There was still something of a man in that face although the lower jaw stretched forward into a crude muzzle. The mouth opened to reveal gleaming fangs. Brown hair covered powerful shoulders that withstood any pounding.

"Stop please," Henry said but the only answer was a bellowing howl. Instead of ripping out his throat, Buck's jaws clamped onto Henry's upper arm. Henry screamed as teeth sank into his flesh. He struggled to pull away, when Buck released his grip.

Henry struggled to focus on the creature that stepped back into the darkness but the pain overwhelmed his senses. He passed out.

When he awoke the sun was low in the sky. He thought it was rising but it was in the wrong part of the sky. How had he slept the entire day?

Movement caught his attention. Buck emerged from the trees, moving on all fours. His form blended into the encroaching darkness. Henry tried to speak but couldn't summon the strength. His chest was soaked with blood. His arm ached. Would Buck kill him now? Why hadn't he been killed already?

As the sun sank lower, Buck seemed to expand to fill the distance between the camp and the trees. His breathing echoed so loudly it drowned out the roaring of Henry's blood. It sounded like a howl. Inside Henry, something stirred. He felt pulled toward that call. He stared harder into the darkness, trying to see Buck, trying to will him closer.

When Buck finally lifted his voice to howl into the sky, Henry opened his mouth to join him.

Writing Critique

Time for them to critique your story. You handed it out two weeks ago. It was so perfectly typed you couldn't even find a typo after you'd photocopied it. In the photocopy place, the guy stapled it for free so it looked crisp and neat. On the clean, white paper with black ink your words seem to jump off the page and you're excited, thinking this is the best thing you've written so far, possibly that you'll ever write and your heart is hammering so hard you feel like it's going to burst and mess up all your internal organs. But it doesn't so you head home to get ready.

You handed it out full of hope, thinking they'll like it, they'll see you in it, even though you tried to allow only your characters to talk. The characters are supposed to have things to say and you wanted to allow them that freedom without prejudice. The group members take it rather casually, your story, your baby, the crisp, white sheets filled with fine, black ink, and stuff it into their assorted bags.

You wait.

It's been two weeks. You're ready. You're not quite so attached anymore, you've written other things. It isn't such a new darling, there are one or two flaws, but you still believe basically it's pretty sound. You're still hopeful. They'll like it, you tell yourself.

The night comes. They arrive smiling and chatting. You believe they enjoyed your work and secretly you congratulate yourself. You wanted them to like it so much, you're happy they did.

You wait patiently through the normal chit chat. Although you're anxious to hear what they have to say you relax into the discussion. You're all friends here, right? After a while, when you're getting nervous, they turn to your story. Their smiles slip a little. You pretend not to notice. They'll have good things to say.

Looking particularly composed, Suzanne begins. Her blonde hair is combed into an attractive coif. Her face, scrubbed clean, has a hint of makeup, playing up the freshness of her skin. She smiles almost apologetically, showing a bit of teeth.

The writing is good, she starts out. Your heart pounds faster, already you hear the "but", it's coming, you feel it, like the ache you get in your neck when the weather is humid because of an old whiplash injury. It tells you when it's going to rain by the sharp biting pain, the dull continuous ache means it's going to stay humid and a slow build-up traces a thunderstorm. This is what you feel now, a thunderstorm, it's in your neck, tightening like rubberbands, pulling your head to one side.

Your plot needs work, she tells you. You blink at this invisible slap but before you can recover she is hitting you again. There's not enough strength in what's happening, the words are passive, there's portions that could be cut out, others need expanding. Your mind is reeling but you try obediently to write it down. You don't protest. You're here to learn after all, here to expand your skills, make them better. You think you're getting a nose bleed.

Mary is next. Quiet and shy, you've always admired the way she manages to paint such unusually vivid characters with such simple phrases. You've watched her steady progress and cheered her onward. Maybe she'll see the inner vision, maybe she'll like it better.

She liked it worse. There's no feeling in it, she tells you. Your head is spinning, are you writing in English? You try to explain it's the character speaking, but she stops you. You have to feel the emotion in order for it to come out. But, you try to say but the moment is gone and she's off, picking out passages for emphasis. You're left with the thought that the character is cut off from her emotions, but you suspect you've forgotten what you're talking about, maybe you never knew. You shut up.

She finishes with a flourish and an admonishment that you'd better start writing with emotion, there hasn't been any so far. You swallow. Your handwriting has deteriorated. You can't read what you've written, but it's ringing in your ears so it doesn't matter. You'll remember it forever.

David steps in. He sits with his hair slicked back and his glasses on perfectly straight. He is so rational, so reasonable, not a thought out of place, not a gesture out of context. He details how you should emphasize aspects and themes you thought were well outlined. He shakes his head and launches into a deep discussion of the techniques of layering abstractions and you get lost after the first sentence. As you continue to jot down notes you feel the pen dig into your fingers leaving grooves in your flesh. A hangnail has split open and a tiny drop of blood has welled up like a bubble waiting to pop.

After the general comments, they go page by page. You notice the whiteness has faded to an offwhite, more off than white. What happened to those newborn photocopies you made? They couldn't be those clumps of paper, held together by a loosened staple.

The sound of pages turning is like a knife drawing slowly across your jugular. You put a hand to your throat. The warm blood rises up over your fingers. The cut seems deep as you try to press it closed, but it won't close. As you fall to the floor, you hear them still talking, building upon each other's comments like a wall. Haven't they noticed you've fallen off the couch? Haven't they noticed the blood staining the carpet?

You close your eyes and feel faint. Someone, you can't tell their voices apart anymore, laughs, a soft, timid laugh that reverberates in your ears until the blood has drained away. By this time, you've saturated the rug. It's soggy and squishy with blood. You blink up at the ceiling, your body miles away. Do I feel anything, you wonder, thinking you're supposed to feel something, after all you're supposed to write with feeling. But you can't even feel your toes, there's no nerve endings left so you lie like a rag doll staring at the ceiling which, you notice could do with some paint, it's faded in the sun. You feel rather faded yourself. The group's words are a low murmur in your ears, like a far away lawnmower on a summer day. I feel nothing, you tell yourself. There is still some blood in your throat. It gurgles.

Afterwards, they leave together, clutching their papers and cackling. They toss your story down beside you. The first one lands with a loud smack and begins to absorb your blood. You turn your head, feeling your hair slide against your skull, so you can watch. Already the blood has soaked through several pages. Other copies land nearby, scattered haphazardly.

You want to stand and walk everyone to the door, after all you're the host. But your legs won't obey, they've become rubber and your arms flap uselessly against the soddened carpet. You see only feet as they walk to the door. David wears sneakers, worn but still serviceable. Mary wears leather loafers and Suzanne wears suede boots, nicely brushed. She probably never gets salt stains, you think fuzzily. They're almost to the door. Their heads are tiny pebbles on top of massive bodies. Their voices float like predatory birds. You can't understand what they're saying. You wonder vaguely if you wrote everything down.

A rising chorus of voices makes you focus your eyes. At the door, they wave goodbye, oversized hands flapping. Another chorus and they vanish, shutting the door.

You blink and remember you should have asked them to stop by the hospital. I'm blood type B negative, you think. You're falling asleep, but before you can get there your brain slaps you.

"Hey," you call out to the empty living room. "When's the next meeting?"

About the Author

Based in Toronto, Canada, Rebecca M. Senese writes horror, science fiction and mystery/crime, often all at once in the same story. Garnering an Honourable Mention in "The Year's Best Science Fiction" and nominated for numerous Aurora Awards, her work has appeared in *Tesseracts 16: Parnassus Unbound, Imaginarium 2012, Tesseracts 15: A Case of Quite Curious Tales, Ride the Moon, TransVersions, Deadbolt Magazine, On Spec, The Vampire's Crypt, Storyteller, Reflection's Edge, Future Syndicate* and *Into the Darkness*, amongst others.

When not serving up tales of the macabre, mysterious or wondrous, she volunteers as a zombie or vampire at haunted attractions in October to stalk and scare all the unsuspecting innocents.

Find Me Online

Website - http://www.RebeccaSenese.com
Twitter - http://twitter.com/RebeccaSenese